I0580448

War No Peace

Cover art by Douglas C. Granum.

Cover design by Scott Norris

douglasgranum.com | monkeyhouse-media.com

ISBN 978-1-939723-23-9

First Edition

DOUGLAS C. GRANUM

War No Peace

T he most hurtful circumstance about sorrow is the way it invites the crowding in of memories of happier times for poignant comparison with one's present misery, and I was miserable.

I was wet, anxiously dancing, shivering really, on a clammy flak jacket in the bottom of a partially flooded foxhole in the north central jungles of Papua New Guinea. Jin Rin, my master, was slumped on the inner edge of our foxhole.

If you know Papau New Guinea, I was south of Madang and northwest of Goroka. The jungles here were mainly estuaries of the mighty writhing rot-brown Sepik River which disgorges down river near the village of Wewak.

It took our squad two weeks along with fifteen native guides to hike into this village of Kamindibit. The village lies in deep jungle off the banks of the crumbling muddy Sepik, about a 30-minute hike.

Let me explain something here: I am the remaining member of our squad of four. Men called me Little Hiro. I am a West Highland white terrier, 13 inches tall with pure white long fleecy hair.

We started this clandestine mission with supreme self-assurance. We stealthily sailed from southern Japan beneath the surface, surfacing only a few times for fuel. Finally, after days of sub surface, we sailed into the sea of Bismarck.

We were in the Emperor's submarine, Kashima Maru, I-52. We appeared from beneath the sea off the north coast of New Guinea. Our goal: to set up a radio listening post in the jungles to transmit messages to ships and subs at sea in the area.

We arrived in a thick sumi ink sea with large yellow globs of moon lighting each glassy roller. We could feel the heated sea through the hull. Sea temperature was 85° Fahrenheit. It was stifling. Coming to a long gliding stop some hundreds of yards off-shore, we very slowly blew air tanks, coming to periscope depth.

We all held our breath for a moment as our captain climbed into the conning tower, standing on the pale green grill. Pulling down the steering handles of the periscope, he looked into the eyepiece and slowly, intently looked around us while slowly walking the periscope around. We all stared up into the tower. He looked down and said,

"Subete kuria." All clear.

Climbing back down from the tower he gave the order to dive to 50 feet. Soon we disappeared from the surface, silent as a seal submerging. We were there, then we weren't, with just a ripple left.

Inside the sub all was warm and cheerful with expectations for great success for our mission.

The captain, a friend of Jin Rin's family back in Edo, announced a party for the young lieutenant and his gallant squad before setting off into the infested night. This party was common knowledge, since there are very few secrets on a submarine.

At this departure party there was much good cheer. They shouted various toasts.

"Tosuto!"

"Kampai!"

The sake was brought into the galley in a generous wooden barrel. The barrel was wrapped in vines. The Kagami-Biraki, or breaking open of the sake barrel, was a well reserved tradition in Japan. On the barrel in green calligraphy, it said "Rokko-oroshi." The captain and Jin Rin both held the wooden ceremonial mallet and together broke open the top of the cedar keg. Small golden square wood cups were passed around while the cook filled the cups again and again with a wooden ladle. There was a lot of sake in the barrel.

There was much real laughter at first, and then to my dog's ears the laughter became more forced. Outside that hull next to me was a heated ocean. Out past that was a jungle island, filled with what? The sub would move on, we would stay, alone.

Our squad was given flags from some of the crew's personal sports clubs, flags signed by the entire crew. Rowing clubs even an archery club, all signed by the crew. The flags and crews were from all over Japan.

We were given special black headbands that said "Hirohito" on them in cream color. The Emperor had signed the first one with a brush pen himself. The captain gave this highly precious headband to Jin Rin. At the party the captain gave one of many toasts to Jin Rin with his square wooden cup. They both held their arms high and toasted again and again. I saw Jin Rin stumble against the galley table.

We were feted for the bold but vital mission we were now embarking on.

At this point the captain pulled out from behind his back an ivory paper wrapped object with a wide red silk ribbon. This saiko no okurimono, this greatest of gifts, was a battle flag from Jin Rin's grandfather who was an Admiral on board the Yamoto, the world's largest battleship. It had been made into a keepsake flag for Jin Rin. The captain and crew created and signed the flag. The white signed background was signed by Jin

Rin's sports club. The red ball was from the Yamoto, the silk of it was from a parachute.

We were given a great feast of fine rich food which, considering we mostly starved on board, was merrymaking. It was a true treat. The cook made sushi. The crew gave us mementos of all kinds.

I was given a t-bone steak which I ended up sharing with the ship's cat, Iyami, something I had never done before. I kind of liked her.

"More sake!" our engineer cried.

Everyone finally at last all yelled hurrah, and then kampai to the Emperor, then broke up and went back into working stations. Over the next ten minutes we got ready to leave the sub forever.

If that thought doesn't scare the hell out of you, I don't know what would.

While the men packed, the captain brought the Kashima to periscope depths once more.

Jin Rin packed his very important ivory handled katana, his samurai sword. The tsuba, or hand guard, was carved with lotus flowers and lotus leaves. Its razor-sharp blade reflected and refracted the dim lights from the interior of the sub. The sword was inlaid with golden florals.

"Who planned this?" my terrier brain wondered.

We were going to set four small black rubber rafts into the sea, climb down off the sub and into the rafts with all of our gear in the open ocean.

New Guinea was known the world over for its coasts, and high lands that were infested with wild men and cannibals. That great seething, slashing death, poison darts guided in flight by colorful dead bird's feathers. There were mock copulations, ritual stabbings, mock spear point attacks at the "Singing Seed", the Adam's apple.

"What could go wrong?" I wondered.

Soon the hatches were un-latched, pushed, and forced open. A small amount of warm water dropped onto our upturned faces. Hot humid air rushed into and around the inside of the sub as if someone had taken a bucket of steam and sloshed the inside of the sub with it.

All of the glass dials, gauges, and eyeglasses were instantly steamed up so that handkerchiefs had to be used to wipe away the moisture.

There were warm, drunken bows, shaking hands, the rare embrace as they packed their last-minute mementos, rechecking their packs. Some men who were next on duty were passed out, heads on hands on the galley tables, not wanting to miss the moment of departure.

The mood was decidedly somber, infinitely incandescent, with false laughs, a tear, a wink.

There were worried looks, sour smells,

low murmurs that sounded like the distant contiguous moaning of death to my canine ancestral sensitivities.

The atmosphere was a cross between an execution, intense forbidding, rot, and garroting, against a coming decapitation.

After all, we didn't know the land at all and the people least of all. We had no idea how to communicate with them. We were, however, heavily armed, extremely well equipped, and disciplined. Despite studying drawings and etchings of some very early books, there was basically nothing to go off of. The maps only said, "Unexplored."

The world knew, however, that this was a real place, set in the far distant past.

Fourteen hours in an airplane would take you from modern man to cave man.

In this world of drums, it paid to know which drumbeat meant "come" and which drumbeat meant "run". You could pay with your life if you didn't.

What was food, what was poison? People were attacked with axes and machetes. Axes with jade blades. Death was everywhere, revered, celebrated. Dead lorikeets hung by their feet on vine belts around dark-skinned men.

Their women had fortress-like dark features, hostile, frightened, deep-set eyes, bodies rubbed with red pig's fat and edgy charcoal. Glistening alive, they reflected burning fires and smelled like smoke.

This was a place where there were spears, bows and arrows, knives, slings, blow guns with poison darts, and poison stakes buried in mud. Fear was real here. It was reasonable to have trepidation here.

There were sharp instruments for killing a wide variety of creatures, including infamously eating their enemies and shrinking their heads by smoking them days and years over smoldering fires, the heads tied high in the smoky rafters, high in special places that were thatched and mysteriously painted.

There was another odd connection in that the smoked heads smelled to me like our missionary smelled at our private temple on our estate in Hiroshima.

It was out into this jungle world we were going and to be left forever, a one-way trip.

Climbing up the coning tower's steel ladder, helping hands pulled others out through the hatch onto the wet slippery rounded black deck.

The men handed me up like a large cabbage, one to the next one, to the next one up, on up till I stood on the wet rounded deck. Next, they handed Big Hiro, our other war dog, up onto the deck.

The air was humid, almost as though there were a mist, which there wasn't. There was no air movement. The surrounding ocean was flat and calm, with rather large smooth rollers.

These large, oily waves rolled up onto the sides of our deck, then roundly rolled off, reflecting the moonlight as it rolled off of the deck.

Jin Rin saluted and bowed lowly to the captain. They each had a last ritual square wooden cup of sake.

"Kampai." Arms high to the Emperor, they dashed down the sake in a swallow while tossing their cups into the glistening golden sea.

We watched as the little wooden cups floated along like a small sacred golden flotilla. Even though the sea was calm, the little square wooden cups went frolicking, rollicking along, dipping and bobbing to some distant current.

Turning to the captain, Jin Rin bowed once more, then turned back to the sea and our raft. He waited, watching the wave pattern until one wave on a high roll looked perfect.

Jin Rin took me, stepped into the bottom of the rubber raft, and we floated off into the sea.

The rafts were held by ropes tied to the sub. The raft jerked and pulled, anxious to be free from the bulk of the sub. As we left from the safety and warmth of the sub, I feared. I carried anxiety into the black rubber raft.

I was terrified.

We were set adrift between the Kashima-Maru and where the coast waited afar off.

The ocean was alive with alien smells. The air smelled intensely sweet with cloying florals and the dying, rotting smell of jungle. Decaying colorful birds, dead crocodiles, rotting trees, and fetid scummy water overcame my senses. The ocean smelled oily from the sub nearby, and then there was the brisk, saline smell of the South Seas.

The moon was huge and full. Our commanders ordered our full moon months in advance so we would have better visibility but not be exposed to daylight.

Pushing off from the huge rolling wet glistening black bulk of the sub, the men all paddled on the port side, turning our raft around and pointing toward the dark distant line of white surf. Between our raft and the breakers were endless gleams of gold rolling to the distant beach, finally fracturing into broken moon beams in the rolling surf.

Hanging over the distant moonstruck beach were tall ghostly palms with an impenetrable black silent forest behind. We saw no campfires, or illumination of any kind.

Beneath the dark dome of the star-filled sky, the full moon's reflection rolled toward the distant white sandy shore on the white glacial crest of each wave. I was brought to my feet when the gentle nature of the waves changed. They began to steepen and grow larger until a few here and there began cresting in anticipation of the shallower seas and surf around the islands.

Just then, Ito, our machine gunner as well as our ground navigator, said,

"Look."

As we crested the next wave, we looked back to where he was pointing to see where the remaining five feet of the Kashima Maru's periscope sliced and shattered the moon's golden tessellated watery path. Slowly the periscope, its great revolving periscopic eye turned toward us, not fifty feet behind us, sent to us a Morse code by electric lamp through the sub's cyclopean glass eye.

"O-N-E M-O-R-E D-A-Y B-E-G-I-N-I-N-G. G-O-O-D L-U-C-K."

We watched with grave trepidation as the K-51 quietly disappeared into the sumi black ink of the sea. We all looked at each other. It had been maybe thirty minutes from the loud warm drunken boil of the sub's raucous goodbye, to Jin Rin and the captain's last goodbye, to this. We were alone, really alone. Jin Rin, who was decidedly drunk, kept giving directions no one could understand, so didn't obey.

Our radio operator, Mr. Kobayashi, was throwing up. He smelled like sour sake, which I had smelled plenty of on our now distant estate near Hiroshima.

Ito was stilled with fear. He stared at the near, dark jungle. Ito now had no shells for his gun since they went to the bottom when his raft flipped in the surf. He said he had a pocketful, as though I would know what that meant. I didn't, but Jin Rin did, swearing loudly at the carelessness of the gunner.

We paddled toward the dark, frothing,

bursting sea where it broke in great moon-light-shattering combers at the face of the sand wall.

It was here at the shore's edge where the sand steepened into a near vertical wall. In many places there were sharp, jagged, exposed palm tree roots sticking out from the sand wall.

Waves continuously crashed, rolling up onto the shore, then quickly sucking back on the steep beach, back out to foaming, roiling sea. The crashing waves caused a low salty ground fog.

Along the shore, some rollers were less crashing. We saw that in places there were underwater rocks and submerged objects that changed the way the rolling surf hit the beach.

We saw some places where the beach was sandy and even, the sand wall at the land end was lower. This looked like as good a place as anywhere we could get off of the beach and up on land without flipping or filling with sea water.

By timing our approach in wave lulls, we saw a way to the beach in the smooth, calmer areas where we even thought we might stay dry doing it, with Jin Rin telling me excitedly, drunkenly, that we could do it, and me excitedly barking.

In one of those roller lulls, Jin Rin paddling, Mr. Kobayashi furiously paddling, everybody surging, smiling, me barking, we sailed smooth as silk through breakers up onto the white sand beach.

Jin Rin piled out headfirst and fell drunkenly, face first in the shallow warm salt water on his knees. Lifting himself up to his hands and knees, staring down, he looked dazed as he watched the receding surf run out between his legs. I jumped out of the raft, running over to Jin Rin, licking him on his salty face.

Mr. Kobayashi, who was terrified even when we were leaving the sub, now stood in the raft, and screamed, pointing. We looked at him, then to where he was pointing.

I barked and started shivering.

I lifted my left front foot in the air and tried to scent this sooty, stringy, black amalgamation of roots, colorful feathered bodies, and doom.

We all looked up, staring in horror. There were many grotesque, black charcoal-rubbed men with jagged lighting painted markings all over their bodies. Their bodies were smeared with red earth, rancid pig fat, and charcoal dust.

Their hair was thick, and formed in fantastic shapes, each different from the next. They had bright feathers, combs, and small bells among many other things stuck into their black kinky hair.

They were a constantly shifting, striated black mass, covered here, all howling and gesticulating with spears and bows and knives in their black hands, all roving and prowling back and forth above us. One man was accidentally shoved over the sand bank, down by us. He screamed and yelled, climbing the shifting sands. People handed him their hands to get him away from us as fast as possible. They were trying to see us, and yet we could also see that they were perhaps afraid of us.

The others tried to get a look at us from on top of the short sand wall by peering down on us. They all had spears and bows with arrows knocked. Long knives were in their waistbands.

Jin Rin, getting up to his feet, stood with his mouth gaped open, vomited up green bile, then gagged. Looking at this hoard, he couldn't talk. Above him he saw, in his drunken state, dozens of fantastically feather-adorned, brightly painted savages. They were gawking at us like small children, jab-bering like small birds.

Jin Rin reached down, grabbed me, and held me close to his chest. Man did that feel good. Let's not kid ourselves, I was not an elephant, and in that crowd, I felt pretty small and endangered, but somehow like a white shaman, significant.

A man in the middle of this riotously painted group was a little chief-like man who did all the talking. He was shorter than Mr. Kobayashi, and Mr. Kobayashi was very short.

The little chief's face was painted yellow and orange. He smiled often; his lips and mouth were red, his teeth and gums were red. He spits globs of red spit. I smelled it when he spit in the sand, it smelled like sour smoke. He talked all of the time, very softly.

Jin Rin discovered that if he moved abruptly, the chief would flare and pull back. Jin Rin also discovered that if he removed his glasses the chief became uneasy.

It turns out that these hideous children of blackness, these ominous, ill-omened specters were afraid of Jin Rin and our squad. They, with spears, arrows, axes, knives, everything murderous and deadly, were frighted and panicked by our little squad.

They were in a sort of tremulous, apprehensive state. This hypnotic state extended to me. They had dogs, but none like me: pure white and somehow from the sea.

They averted their eyes and wouldn't look at me. This made me nervous, or should I say more nervous than I already was.

To say the very least it was scary beyond belief for a small shaman-like white dog like me.

It was like me and a neighbor's dog in Hiroshima. He was bigger and a whole lot physically stronger, but I had to be smarter, and I was. My first rule for all dogs: don't yap.

These wild, crazed natives had dogs strung up over fires, smoking them to eat. In one village we passed through I saw three human heads smoking with the dogs' heads and whole bodies. There were carved trees and hideous masks. These people reeked of rot; they rubbed red dirt laden pig fat over their grunting jungle bodies. When they tried to pick me up, Jin Rin and our squad were there to protect me.

We finally got off that beach. We hiked inland for a few hundred meters when we hit a wide, well-used pathway through the overhanging jungle. Turning uphill to the right, we began hiking.

The pathway was a totally rutted bush track in a sea of mud and footprints of pigs, dogs, and people. Everywhere we went new people would join us and others would leave.

We passed legions of walking hill people with bila bags for carrying loads slung on their backs, while on their heads they carried loads of wood. Pigs were everywhere, traveling with their owners. The mountains and valleys were a kind of paradise with gardens, great masses of flowers and fruits.

These people are unlike any I have ever seen, never in Japan. Their faces so dark and wild, faces with deeply inset eyes, dark black eyes punched into 50,000 years of time. Great, huge grinding jaws meant for ripping and tearing flesh and coarse vegetables.

Their bodies, unlike the Japanese, were short, powerful, and thick, with quick eyes, a ready smile.

Men, as menacing as death, coyly holding each other's little fingers, smiling shyly as young virgins.

As the men walked, they were endlessly preening, prancing, boldly looking at us to know if we saw how magnificent they were. They all wore a large variety of body paints and tattoos. Some of them wore only white clay. Women in morning had faces of green, only green. Some faces were blue, some purple, red, or yellow, all held in place with layers of pig fat.

Here in this place, I again, for some strange reason, remembered our missionary and our little chapel on our estate in Hiroshima.

These people reminded me of the cross with the dead man nailed to it in our chapel at home. I felt death everywhere, in abstract ways that reached way past my daily consciousness.

Voodoo magic, JuJu, dark thoughts. The detritus of the beautiful jungle, the green hills and valleys, the rushing rivers, cloudy, mist capped mountains, all poured out through rivers and rivets, their blood and carnage.

Dying birds hung gasping on sticks. Owls, heads hanging down, tied by their feet to their owner's belt, occasionally struggled feebly to free themselves. Parrots pierced with small sticks, drying. Bird feathers of every color and shape. The feathers, beautiful and fragile, waved gayly above black and green ochre faces.

Thunderous snakeskin drums challenged the sun to the right to shine, so throbbing to my sensitive ears.

Skins of small quiet jungle canopy cats, silent in their night, hung fully clawed and gutted between lactating pig-rubbed women's breasts.

Beaks of primordial hornbills, horrible in their form, danced death far from their bodies.

We dogs are known for our sensitivities, and what I continually felt with this black mass of primitive people was their elevation of the splendor of death. It was their game, a serious game. The arrows, quick ancient eyes, challenging and fearful, though one afternoon we saw two tribes ready for war with one another, and then it started to rain. No one wanting to get their outfits wet, all went home to fight another day.

This great Stone Age assemblage, some chanting, some bouncing, some stamping, ebbed and flowed around us as we passed villages and met groups on the well-trodden trails.

Some of the men were covered in white owl feathers and hissed when they walked.

For the last day and night, we had been hiking steadily up through heavy rain with sodden bright birds sitting, brooding under large dark green leaves in the dripping jungles. Humidity, heat, and hot rain left all of us dripping and exhausted.

Smells of hyacinth, gardenia, and orchids floated by from the jungle, fresh green smells side by side with deeply rich rotting odors, dank festering smell of dying and re-birth.

We had about twenty savages with us at most all times. Sometimes they went off, returning later with a snake or a lizard, a bright bird, sometimes mushrooms that glowed in the dark.

The jungle floor and the trees were alive with food if you knew how to get it. One time one of our guides brought us a monkey with the blow gun dart still in the monkey's neck.

The jungle was filled with the raucous calls of screaming birds and the rumbling thunder of lizard skin drums. Some drums were sharp, clear and near, others rumbled in hollowed logs from a great distance.

There were great extended pathways between these mountains, rivers, and oceans. Along the well-used trails we passed other savages, children, and mothers. Sometimes there were tribes of young warriors who were rude and threatened us with spears.

Our group went on while our smiling little orange chief roughly pushed others away from us on the trail and in the villages. As we continued, we came around a bend and came upon a small pool and river. In the water of the dark pool was a woman submerged up to her neck. Her hair was black and curly. In her arms she held a small glossy wet jet-black child. When she moved, the water polished her wet breasts.

Behind her on the riverbank at the base of a small hill was a grass hut on stilts. In front of it was a small fire with poles for drying the few little fish that hung there. All around the mother and child were birds: white egrets, small pileated egrets, ducks, eagles, parrots, birds of all kinds.

We finally arrived at the village of Kamindibit after hiking through jungles for days. We only succeeded in finally reaching Kamindibit by brutalizing the savages by force and terror.

Once Jin Rin discovered that the natives were terrified of him, he made them bid his every command. He was very disrespectful to them, and they cowered.

Truth be told had it not been for the natives we would never have had the remotest chance of finding Kimindabit. Why they obeyed us when they could have so easily killed us, I didn't know.

We hiked over high, mist covered mountain passes down steep slippery vine laced trails to raging rivers below which we often crossed by vine bridges.

We passed through several villages where the differently dressed natives threatened our packers.

Our guide, the smiling little orange and yellow painted chief with the bone through his nose, was a mountain man from the mountains of the Iran Jaya.

He married a woman from the river

village and consequently was living in Kamindibit, a river village. It was, of course, this village where we hoped to set up a radio sending unit.

The little chief was able to protect the coastal men in his group and us. Since he passed this way often, he spoke many languages, so everyone trusted and liked him.

He wore a little couscous fur hat, had tattoos, braided wrist, and ankle bands, and was naked, except he had his prized possession, his penis, inserted into a long seed pod which was then tied to his shoulder.

As we hiked deeper into the forested mountains, the bird-like little chief started to hold Jin Rin's little finger with his own callused little finger, a sign of special friendship. Jin Rin didn't much like this, since even as a little boy he hadn't like to be touched too often.

We arrived at the village of Kamindibit on a large bend in the squirming, tortuous bowels of the brown Sepik River. We had arrived from upriver, from the village of Tembuki. We arrived in the early morning dark to avoid detection by American spotter planes.

Paddling with the current, our orange and yellow chief was in the bow with a large search light. Occasionally he swept the surface of the river to the bank of the river. There were always the eyes of crocodiles protruding just above the surface of the dark Sepik.

On what looked to me like any and every other riverbank, we slowly nosed up to a low log pier in almost total darkness.

Our little chief handed someone on the pier a rope, who tied it to the pier. We slowly swung all the way around with our bow fastened to the log. The flow of the river brought us around to rest against the long log that served as a dock.

Next, a notched log that stood nearby

extended up about ten feet into the early morning dark.

Many people were standing and looking down at us, talking excitedly with the men in our canoe. Jin Rin forced the natives to carry all of our gear to the village.

Striking out on the well beaten trail, we walked for about thirty minutes, finally arriving at a beautiful little pond connected to a river.

Built on and around the pond were bare wood huts on stilts out over the pond. They were all thatched and dry. Made with bamboo and branches, they were held together by vines and lashings.

Behind the pond I noticed a trail that followed behind a main thatched building, then disappeared up a mountainous track with heavy jungle hanging over it.

Walking through the village on paths that passed over logs and small creeks, we arrived and were honorably given the little yellow and orange chief's own house to sleep in. As we arrived his family was climbing down and going off into another shelter.

The hut was built on post stilts, some five meters in height, out over a small pond. I noticed that there were lots of squirming green baby alligators in the scummy pond water beneath.

There were very few belongings in the tree house. In the middle was a box like structure filled with sand. In the sand a small fire was smoking and over it hung some undistinguishable pieces of meat.

Above the fire in the high ceiling area, were several severed human heads, smoked and shrunken. Also smoking with the human heads were several river fish. The floor was green bamboo poles laid side by side. The whole interior was open to the weather on one side. There were spears and arrows tied in bundles on the wall. There were carvings of men with great penises that would make any dog envious, and carvings of cormorants, the type we used for fishing on the coasts of Japan. There were no lights, the hut was alive in shadows.

Occasionally a lizard would run across the floor, or a brightly colored bird would fly, calling raucously to the roof top. The village was quiet except for the constant jabbering and pointing at our team. Drums rolled constantly; light grey smoke filled in the area over the pond.

We looked around and started to unpack what little we had been able to carry from the disastrous flipping of our rafts in the surf.

The two rafts that flipped had almost all of our clothes and food, plus sustaining gear like spare parts for the radio, bug repellent, diarrhea pills, toothbrushes, toiletry items, and towels. No toilet paper.

We had next to no food, only a minute

amount of rice, some soy sauce, a couple of tins of rice crackers, and some tin fish, along with ammunition for guns that were now at the bottom of the sea of Bismarck. Food was going to be a major problem.

On the good side, the hut high in the air on stilts would be a perfect tower for radio reception. Inasmuch as everything was damp, the bigger miracle would be if we got our radio to work. The short time we had been in the jungle, the wires and connectors and batteries all had begun to corrode.

Jin Rin was now sober and seething with anger, at me, at our whole crew, because nothing has gone like he expected it to.

We walked around looking for a tree to set up our antenna, followed by the whole village. Jin Rin didn't like these people. Twice they nearly captured me. I bit one man until he bled.

It seemed to me that these people killed

those whom they honored most and ate those they hated the most.

Back in our tree house, we got ourselves ready for a much-needed rest. Our food would soon run out, and so we were semi-starving while partly existing on jungle food provided by the natives, which gave all of us the runs.

The little chief, smiling broadly, brought us a large smoked lizard and some roasted lizard eggs on a large jungle leaf. It smelled pretty good in my starved condition.

Jin Rin looked at it in disgust. He screamed at the little chief, in Japanese,

"Kono Baka!" (you moron) Then threw it all to the alligators beneath our hut. The little orange and yellow painted chief smiled shyly, unhappily at the destruction of his personal gift of food. Food in the jungle was hard to get.

Exhausted, sweating, and angry, we sat around on reed mats, toasting, shouting,

"Kanpai," with the small amount of sake that we still had with us. We toasted to the "Sun," our glorious Emperor Hirohito, all without much energy.

We had little idea what tomorrow would bring. No food, no radio, no way out of here, and if we found some way, to where?

None of our plans included a way home. We all planned on our leaders and planners to get us out when our mission was completed. It was now apparent that our mission wouldn't be completed, because in all likelihood we wouldn't get it started.

We were all in a tree house in the jungle, surrounded by headhunters, while American and Australian troops searched for us.

We gradually, fearfully settled down, men on the run. This country we were in seethed with spies and inspired helplessness.

Mr. Kobayashi put our shoes outside

our door, at the bottom of the ladder to our tree house as we always did at home. Bowing low on our knees, we said our prayers to our Emperor. We took our pistols and the few rifles we had, clutching them close to our despondent bodies and lay down, passing out. We were spent and entered a troubling sleep.

As I curled up at Jin Rin's feet on top of his mat, I could hear the thrashing of the leather bills in the jungle. I could hear and smell the sounds of the village around us. I could hear our men snoring. Finally, rolling left, then right, then standing up and shaking, then laying back down again, I finally slept.

I awakened early in the morning. The jungle was alive with activity. Birds of all kinds squawked and whistled while the smell of smoke drifted through the grass walls of our hut. Crocodiles in the river water beneath us hissed.

The village was active. Many people had come earlier to sit on their haunches, waiting for us to wake up and come outside so they could stare at us. Their smaller children stood behind them, staring out. Some smaller ones yet stood inside the thatch skirts, inside of their mother's cloths.

We prepared to fix our small rice breakfast. Mr. Kobayashi, our radio operator, went down the ladder to get the shoes and some water for rice.

Mr. Kobayashi's face was stricken as he climbed back up and told Jin Rin the horrid news.

"What's the matter, Mr. Kobayashi? Say something."

Jin Rin's boots were gone!

This was a major catastrophe since all of Jin Rin's other cloths were lost in the overturned rubber raft in the heavy surf, including his spare boots. This village of stone age people had never seen boots.

Angrily, insanely shouting, Jin Rin ran back into the hut, bringing out his ancient ivory handled family katana. Climbing down the ladder, he confronted the natives who were squatting around, who were always around. Now, seeing Jin Rin's anger and sword, they instantly all jumped to their feet while fingering their great slashing bush knives, making at the same time a huge, powerful exhaling "ooof" sound.

Jin Rin stopped in a classic Samurai pose and unsheathed the gleaming crescent-shaped killing instrument.

Jin Rin advanced, threatening, demanding the return of his boots through sign language and red-faced screaming.

I knew him, he was petrified.

He ultimately prevailed by pointing to his feet and yelling in Japanese, which of course no native could understand, but they understood the screaming, maddened anger, and the polished glistening katana.

Pointing to his bare feet, he demanded his shoes back.

They understood sharp things, like the glistening sword, pointed things, brutal blunt things. They were a soft-spoken people, ferocious jungle warriors, but Jin Rin was insane, a big difference. Jin Rin was in a foaming, frothing rage, screaming. They all pulled back away from this yellow demonic specter.

The little yellow and orange smiling chief, now insecurely smiling, childlike, shouted to one of his men who went running off. Soon he came back, walking slowly, and gave Jin Rin back his boots.

They were destroyed. They had been boiled and had shrunk. They had been cut in pieces, some leather parts of the boots had been chewed and had teeth marks. They were completely ruined forever. The natives were very still, like birds in cover.

Their eyes rolled in terror, some drooling. They mouthed fear, some quiet as instant death, slipped slowly, ever so slowly and patiently, sliding their bare feet in the grass before turning and running away into the jungle.

The whole village had tried to eat the boots. Being cannibals, they had chewed and chewed and chewed, but with no luck.

Having never seen boots of canvas and rubber, or boots of any kind before, they thought that Jin Rin had put his real feet out that night.

Jin Rin stood there in that tense, now hushed jungle in his bare-naked feet with mud squishing up between his toes. All was quiet, so quiet that I looked up and moved closer to him. His eyes began to tear, his face became contorted, his mouth became distorted. I remember that look from when he was a little boy back on our estate in Hiroshima. A tantrum was coming. When he looked like that as a boy, I would run behind Iyami, his mother, for protection.

A civilized man used to shoes who suddenly found himself in those jungles without shoes was a cripple. The jungle floor was alive with spiders, lizards, thorns, fire ants, and bacteria. The mud was fungal ladened. Having no shoes, then attempting to walk without months of acclimation, was disaster.

Standing there in that village clearing, we all looked at Jin Rin to see what would happen next.

At this precise moment of ghastly feng shui, tensions had grown to such a proportion that some disaster had to occur. Someone, something, anything had to pay.

Jin Rin stopped shrieking and calmly stepped forward with his left foot, while lifting the great razor-sharp lotus samurai sword.

Holding aloft this ancient hand-forged weapon, the pride of generations in his family, he planted his feet in the classic ojigi pose, holding his family sword high above his head with two hands, his fingers tightly intertwined and locked. In a lightning-rapid side slashing movement, in one brilliant, flashing kiri kizu, shouting,

"Kiri-sute!" Jin Rin decapitated the little smiling chief, our friend.

The chief instantly dropped straight down, his headless shoulders spurting dark red blood, his bodiless head rolled down and into a small muddy puddle, still grinning.

Pandemonium and insane disbelief caused the whole tribe to begin to sway and howl. They formed their mouths in large ovals, like a howler monkey, and hooted and howled.

"OOOf OOOf OOOf," they all cried. "OOOf."

They were shaking weapons at Jin Rin, screaming, then quickly, in mass, they rushed for the safety and cover of the jungle as Mr. Kobayashi, shot one of the natives who was rapidly advancing on Jin Rin with an ax.

We could hear them, screaming, crying, thrashing, yelling, tearing up plants and breaking others. They knew death, they felt death, they lived with death every moment of the day.

Coming to the plant filled edge of the jungle nearby, they began to accurately throw rocks at us from the camouflaged forest. Drums, great log drums began to reverberate with greater rapidity through the canyons and ridges. There were also the urgent popping sounds of the smaller snake-skin drums closer by.

A spear landed, nearly impaling Jin Rin's bare foot.

Our men hurried, frantically making

Jin Rin a pair of booties from canvas sacks and put dry grass inside while tying them at his ankle.

We grabbed the few things we could carry while rushing, running, panting out of breath up that nearest jungle path I had seen before. Where we were headed to, we had not a clue.

The radio operator, Mr. Kobayashi, shot two more natives trying to stop us. Our midshipman, Ito, saved us by staying back behind and occasionally firing a shot down the trail behind us in the hopes of scaring them. Mr. Ito took an arrow while guarding our flight. He was hit in the stomach and was in much pain. To Mr. Ito's credit, the natives never caught us. They had never seen or heard guns before.

A stick that kills at a great distance is a grave source of magic. The only one with that kind of power was "Big Pella, um belong mix-master". That would be the Christian god Jesus.

After climbing high into the darkening jungle in misty rain we finally ran nearly out of daylight. Fortunately, the dark came, since we were totally spent. No food, no rest, the jungle filled with natives who were intent on killing and eating us, maybe not in that order.

We were petrified.

Mr. Ito has started to spit up dark blood, his urine was also red.

Carefully stepping off the path to avoid footprints, we came up a large antique Kapok tree about 35 meters off the main path. This old giant had natural mossy beds in the crotches of its branches. We slept in this tree, four meters up and 35 meters off the main path. This tree was a huge leafy umbrella. Its great branches were immense. It dripped in lichens and mosses. It was concert hall filled with singing birds, this massive tree was alive in Chinese red, cobalt blue, iridescent green, brilliant yellow, lorikeets. They were in constant motion while warbling and singing.

Here we ate a small portion of what little food we still had. Rice crackers with a minute amount of soy sauce, a dozen grains of rice. In a canteen Jin Rin had scooped crystal clear water from a deep boulder filled mountain creek. The water crashed and fell around us as we made our way across holding to a long vine with our hands and sliding our feet on another vine.

The next morning after eating leaves and grass and a minute amount of raw rice we hiked higher up onto the top of a bald ridge. From here, high up on this ridge, we sat for a few moments in the warm sun. From up here we could see the ocean far off down a distant valley. For once it wasn't raining or misting or foggy. We tried to see the ocean, the river, a valley, or low pass, but we saw nothing. Just endless ridge and low misty clouds, and then again and again more of the same.

Sitting in the sun in silent warmth, Jin Rin said what we all knew: we were utterly lost!

Jin Rin took the crude bandages off Mr. Ito to expose the wound to the healing benefits of the sunshine and fresh mountain air.

We had ryokans, country spas with hot springs, where people were cured from illnesses through special waters, sunshine, and air. My mistress, Jin Rin's mother, and I went to a ryokan with Jin Rin when he had tubercular problems. He was much cured and improved when he came home.

Each of us sat silently in the warm sun, thankful for once not to be moving. Far down in the valleys we could hear birds calling.

I thought about my purple silk bed on its little carved legs on our estate in Hiroshima.

Sitting there in the clear mountain air out on that ridge was heaven itself. There was enough of a light warm breeze to keep away the constant stinging insects. We all lay back in the deep grass, closing our eyes.

Just as I curled my tail over my eyes, I heard an ugly grating sound that seemed to penetrate all the hills and valleys around. I jumped to my feet, barking to awaken my squad. My barking awakened them all in an instant.

Jumping up, they heard the same horrible sound I had heard moments before. It took less than a second when a P-38 twin engine fighter appeared, rising seemingly out of the ground and out of a steep canyon right below and directly in front of us. He came straight up and upon us so fast that we had no time to think of hiding, only wincing. He strafed us and was so close I could see the pilot. He missed us, all of us except Mr. Ito, who took a .50 caliber round in his chest, cutting him in half. His hot blood and body parts were splattered on all of us.

We ran for jungle cover as we watched over our shoulders, the droning plane banking sharply, far out over a deep jungle canyon. He dropped beyond our line of sight for a moment, then seemingly burst up from the ground and roared, screaming over the ridge right at us once more.

Its powerful twin engines making a loud moaning sound, he thundered by us at tree top level while we hid in the jungle. The sound of the P-38's deafeningly loud engines slowly died out little by little, then disappeared in and among the endless mountains and valleys.

As the harsh industrial sound of the P-38 disappeared, we could once again feel the vibrations and hear the incessant rolling sound of the native drums. The drums filled in all gaps.

We heard people shouting from one

mountain to another mountain across the bottomless obscure canyons. The valleys were tracked heavily by hordes of broad, flat bare feet. There were shrines made of the dead and dying, twisted in strangulation, some still fighting Shinigami, the Grim Reaper.

Cloudy mist was everywhere in a thousand forms, climbing, falling, flowing, disappearing and appearing, clouds of mist where mountain tops looked like islands in the Sea of Japan.

This afternoon, while hiding in thick jungle, we decided to wait even longer for it to get a bit darker before we moved. Something had spooked Mr. Kobayashi, our radio operator, so we waited for it to turn dusky.

Sitting in cover yesterday we saw across on another ridge an American patrol, armed to the teeth, of about twenty men.

This evening while waiting for a bit more dark, while just sitting here in the crotch of this large tree, we saw out on the main trail a line of black armed men, silently loping in the direction we had just come from. The hackles on my back came up. These were natives.

Waiting for them to run pass, we picked up our things. We angled down in a cross-country angle going the opposite direction from that which the natives had taken.

While hiking cross country back to the main trail, our radio operator was silently hit in the face by a very brightly colored feathered poisonous frog dart. He winced and pulled the dart out. Around the point of entry his skin began to redden.

His face almost immediately began to swell. In about 30 minutes his head was near twice its normal size. His eyes were swollen shut and his mouth looked like a cut dried apple from Iyami's pantry.

His moans were piteous. He cried for

his wife. We lead him by the hand for a short while. When he couldn't walk, we carried him until he stiffened and started spasmodically jerking, his heart pounding itself to death as he died, racked with dread. His eyes were deep pools of horror.

I was looking up at my master, Jin Rin, who sat opposite me in our tiny fetid foxhole. His head hung down and his skinny arms rested on his legs with his bony white hands covering his knees. He looked yellow, he looked defeated, he looked exhausted.

His looks at me were morose, dejected, and inquisitive, his body smelled terrified. We had hiked two days, almost all downhill to this foxhole we had dug here near the coast. We could hear the surf. We heard someone shouting in Japanese last night. We saw many American ships out to sea from the mountain tops. Now amongst the jungle drums were the ships cannons, howitzers, machine guns, pistols and rifles, the insistent roar, the gnashing sounds of war.

I was Jin Rin's eyes, ears, and nose. I was a war dog. My role was to protect my squad.

I scanned the dripping, malevolent, cavernous black jungle once again. Every sound was a potential symptom of violent death. Simple things, the snap of a twig, the slap of a branch against a jacket, a cough or sneeze, the smell of American cigarettes, all could bring swift death for what they portended.

In amongst this death were large pendulous yellow orchids, great flowered red spires alive with ants, thick floral scents, something that reminded me of our gardens on our estate. All these gorgeous scents wafted through the thick menacing air. The rot of something dead or dying hung heavily everywhere in the thick jungle air. Everything was dying or being killed, they rotted, they stank, the smell of growth.

I was decidedly hungry and beyond thirsty, our last morsel of food was yesterday, stale soy-soaked rice crackers. We had not had real food for days.

Someone once said that people who died from starvation all ended up looking alike in death. I thought to myself that starving in this place was the least violent way to die here.

My last drink was lapping urine and blood laced water from the muddy bottom of our shallow foxhole. We don't know what we would drink or eat or do or feel like when we are starving. I didn't want to know what I looked like, how I felt was bad enough.

Desperation reined.

There was no dry place to sleep. In fact, there hadn't been a dry place to sleep in weeks.

Jin Rin's foot, which was still in a bag, had become infected; it smelled. His skin peeled since his foot was constantly damp and wet.

The oppressive jungle wept, steaming in what little sun comes out, reeking at night with decay. Flowing water was everywhere, even, it seemed, up from the ground. The ground was wet and muddy, the sky was wet and muddy, they mirrored each other, a dirty photograph.

Leeches, spiders, and immense rain-washed shiny black crabs were everywhere. Jin Rin wrenched down his soaking wet flight pants and pulled off blood sucking leeches. His foot coverings that the squad made for him were in constant need of repair. He walked with a limp.

He was petrified with blinding fright, sometimes he just stared in fearful disbelief at Ito, his cadet school buddy and former ground navigator, now lying dead. Before Mr. Ito was shot, he and Jin Rin took turns holding each other's head out of the water in the foxhole so the other could sleep.

"Time and events rob us of all."

It had turned to a pitchy, bitter dusk, here and there a bit of sun shown in the broken clouds. Jungle sounds were close, very near while boiling jungle rain fell in sheets. The final sunset was out a few moments ago, slicing the grey clouds like a golden samurai sword.

The little bit of sky that I could see in that instant was tangerine and blue. Flocks of orange and indigo parrots and yellow and red parakeets were all flying over in neon terraformations.

All had changed, deep sunset with the distant sun only a reddish line over the distant ocean.

Near the equator the sun had dropped like a kabuki stage curtain. A scimitar of a moon shown, disappeared, and shown again and again before finally vanishing, devolving to rainy impenetrable black.

Close and fetid in the gathering and fearfully projecting darkness I heard the rasping sound of the great leather bill's coarse wings rubbing against the leaves nearby in the very dangerous jungle as it settled in to roost for the night.

All birdsong ceased with the darkness except for two owls singing their same song over and over and over until I thought I was going to go nuts. The owl, or "fukuro," was said to bring our people luck against disaster, but I was not feeling lucky in that moment. In fact, just the opposite.

Lying, thrashing, and squirming beside me was Big Hiro, the only other dog in our small former squad of four. Big Hiro moaned and cried. He has been shot by Jin Rin Matabushido, my master. Jin Rin shot Big Hiro, then he turned with fear gazed madness, leveling his Nambu 94, the so-called suicide pistol, on me. He was crying and yelling,

"Shizukani shiro, Little Hiro, shut up," as he waved the Nambu in my face.

I stood dead still, Jin Rin's eyes were crazed, his hair was wet and plastered against his pale sweating brow. He was raving.

As his eyes frantically roved the dark jungle around us, he occasionally shivered then murmured,

"Iyami," his mother.

I knew her well; she was charming and very far away. On many afternoons I sat on her lap in her exquisite bamboo garden as she absentmindedly pet my little white head.

She stared off, listening to the crickets in a small delicate bamboo cage hanging from the pendulous katsura tree nearby. During these quiet moments in her gracious floral garden, she told me stories of her husband who was an Admiral on the gigantic battle ship "Yamato".

She told me about Jin Rin when he was a little boy. He was always nervous, she said.

She looked into my eyes and said,

"Perhaps, Dear, you wouldn't remember about the time we took him to the Ryokan for his breathing, but even though he got better, he has never been 100 percent."

I, of course, remembered, and I knew about the 100 percent part.

That was the part that now had me feeling utter despair, without leadership.

At those long-ago times she fed me little dainty bits of sweet bean curd, a minute nothing of whipped cream from her exceedingly long painted fingernail, a small grouse leg with soy. I didn't like to admit it, I was spoiled in those days, but now, no, now that was all over. I knew I was in grizzly bear country up to my neck in ussuris.

Some nights, when I could sleep, I still barked and moaned, my legs jumping and running, and then Jin Rin would wake me up to keep me quiet. When he awoke me, I, for just a moment, could still smell the sweet summer grass of our garden and the fresh salt air of Hiroshima.

This sweaty night, unlike many others, was quiet, though there was still the occasional burst of machine gun fire. Back in the inky dark someone screamed in Japanese,

"Kotchi, over here!" and then a grenade.

Jin Rin was babbling loudly at me again. He didn't need to shout at me, humans often forgot that we of the dog family had very acute hearing. A whisper worked as well as or better than a shout.

Jin Rin was frightened; I could hear it in his voice. He was afraid that Big Hiro and I would make a noise and the enemy would find him. The bursting grenade made Jin Rin moan.

His ground navigator lied desperately slumped against the sandy, grainy sides of

the shallow foxhole, his eyes opened, staring, his fires out, dead. His rigid hand was
held high, clenching a dagger, frozen in
place by the breath of "Shinigami", the angel of death.

When the navigator was first shot, I
crept up to him and smelled the wounds,
then I licked them, thinking perhaps I could
make him better. It didn't help. Earlier he
had taken two sniper rounds, BANG BANG,
in his neck. Quietly he pumped, pulsed,
jerked, jumped, and bled in spurts out into
the foxhole. My feet, at first the bright red of
fresh steaming blood, were now black from
the navigator's stale, coagulated blood.
He died instantly. Jin Rin screamed while
scrabbling backwards as far away from the
navigator as he could get in that sad small
wet flooded foxhole.

Normally, back in Japan on our estate
near Hiroshima, Mr. Matabushido, as the
servants called him, was kind of a young

emperor to all of us on the estate. He was gentle.

Jin Rin, which was what I thought of him as, was a Seventh Generation Kenma-suta, a sword master. Everywhere he went I went with him. He inspired respect, and we were inseparable. I slept with him with my head on his silk white pillow on his tatami mat. I rode behind him on the rump of his great white horse, so given this it seemed natural that when he sailed for war in the South Pacific, that I, trained by Jin Rin to be a warrior dog, would naturally sail with him. I was trained to execute a host of difficult maneuvers. I could crawl on my white belly for a mile, I learned a new language, that was communications. Never were communications so vital than in war. I was taught to point out dangerous situations with my eyes and my nose, my sense of smell, and hearing. We terriers had exceptional senses.

Jin Rin's friends scoffed, deriding the

presence of a little dog such as myself at war.

"Why that runty dog doesn't weigh more than two pounds."

I wasn't runty, I was big for my breed. My hair was glossy and pure white. Jin Rin used to laugh and say he could find me anywhere because of my whiteness.

"Look at how small his teeth are." With this, goddamnit, some noble or other would lean down and pick me up, and then try, what the hell, to pull back my lips with their dirty tobacco-stained fingers to look at my teeth. I had my pride, I bit them until they bled. Small doesn't mean helpless. It doesn't mean that every schoolboy or stump dumb noble that comes along dragging a mallet can have their way with me.

Jin Rin's father, Shiki Kenju, who was tutored in calligraphy by the emperor's own tutor, use to tell Jin Rin,

"Remember my young son, courage

grows strong at a wound." No one had heard from Admiral Shiki Kenju, everyone was frightened to talk of him for fear of "fuun," bad luck!

Some other civilian from time to time would ask Jin Rin,

"Why take that dog to war?"

Why? I could answer that myself: because of my senses. Right then I could smell the enemy, they didn't smell like we Japanese, and they were infiltrating.

The heated rain had stopped for the moment and the sopping jungle dripped menacingly, so much so that I couldn't tell if it was enemy infiltration or innocent rainwater running off gigantic crenelated jungle leaves.

These little sounds drove me to distraction, I was the guard dog, and in the dripping jungle I couldn't tell one subtle sound from another.

The cloyingly sweet and putrid humid

air shouted danger to me. I could smell the pungent rank sweat of the creeping menacing white enemy nearby.

Humans forgot a lot about us dogs if they ever knew anything to start with. The fact was most people knew very little about how we thought, how we heard, how we scented the world around us, how we could love, how we could hate when mistreated. We were not little people, rather we came from a long and equally distinguished family as humans. It was not an exaggeration to say that without us dogs, humans would never have gotten so far so fast in this world.

I heard a branch snap in the damp gloom. I looked at Jin Rin, he didn't hear it.

Where was I, oh yes, we terriers loved people, however we are not people. The relationship between us dogs and humans were a bond going back to the beginning of time. If you wished to understand the story of our beginning, step out into a wilderness some night, and listen to the sobbing of a wolf. Now that is a story told.

Love, there is a type of love that gives everything, yet asks nothing. My great, great, great, Grandfather Buto was of this type.

When Buto's old master Tomio-O died, Tomio-O was the benefactor of the famous Golden Tsutakwaa Temple. This temple was on the straits of Itsukushima, Tomio-O was very wealthy and an icon in Japan.

On the day after his death, Buto followed the funeral procession to the temple where his old Master Tomio-O was to be placed in a carved and sculptured niche with carved, marble stone Palace Dogs on each side. The funeral procession was long and winding, with priceless wafting incense, flutes, gongs, holy words, colorful flags, and streaming banners. The family following loudly, wailing, handing out koden, condolence money.

With incense still smoldering in the decorated bronze censor, the elaborate ceremonies finally over, the formal and somber crowd left in tears and resignation. Buto stayed.

He was finally scooped up by a family member, taken back to the castle where later that night he crept out, setting off along the seafront lanes, running by anchored and tied up fishing boats, past net covered dark piers, and around the great white piles of empty oyster shells.

He ran for the Temple again and there, lifting his small white muzzle to the sky, he stayed, howling and moaning, beside his master's grave, until he died five days later of starvation. He had refused to eat. Some said he died of a broken heart. We Highland terriers were known for our strength, but then, goddamnit, no one could live forever with a broken heart, not even a powerful little terrier like Buto, my great, great, great, grandfather.

As our family's ancient patriarch said: "Midnight shakes the memory."

Darkness was now everywhere,

sadness was slashing and pointed.

By now our hopes and dreams of fame for Japan and glory for our Emperor were shattered. Only Jin Rin and I were left.

Sitting, shaking uncontrollably, shivering in the fetid water, I raised my nose and smelled once more the sickeningly sweet stink of the enemy. It was getting stronger. The ghastly stench swirled everywhere in the damp, decaying jungle.

Just on the other side of the ragged, torn lip of our foxhole was death, I could clearly sense it. I could also hear the enemy moving somewhat noisily in the darkness of the jungle nearby.

The rain started again, drumming the tops of the gigantic dark green leaves, distorting the scent in the air.

Something else, I could now detect the smell of another dog. Not Big Hiro, who now had died. I would miss him. He was loyal, what was he killed for?

I looked up at Jin Rin, softly whining as I had been trained to do by him. I then quietly pointed my nose in the direction of the approaching enemy, then looked back at Jin Rin. I did this several times, the water from his helmet dripping on my face as he looked deep into my brown eyes.

Noticing my warning, he quietly, slowly, ever so silently took off his helmet, reached down inside his quilted jacket, and pulled out his glasses, then he put them on.

Even when he was a little boy, he had poor vision. He always wore thick round silver rimmed glasses.

I was his vision, day and night. Without his glasses he was nearly blind. When we were in Japan on our estate, he would sometimes hold me up in the air above his head so I could locate our cattle for him by pointing them out to him with my nose.

He reached down, slowly picked up his Nambu-94, and silently cocked it.

At that exact moment when he put on his glasses the last low dirt-purple clouds suddenly parted, and just for that instant the full moon shone brilliantly clear. Crouching lowly, Jin Rin seized this moment of moonlight to crouch higher, peering over the edge of the shallow foxhole into the dim and dark jungle. It always dripped. The world outside of our foxhole was wet, filled with disturbing pockets of blackness, the end of time on earth.

Here, he thought fortunately, was his moment of bright moonlight to perhaps spot the enemy.

How can we tell how much time we have left on this earth? Wherever you are, I am positive it is shorter in jungle warfare.

I heard a snap, then a whizzing sound,

then Jin Rin gasped like he was going to say something to me, when suddenly he collapsed backward into the flooded foxhole, his head only a foot or so away from where I crouched.

He opened his eyes for an instant, looked at me warmly, and said,

"Oh, Little Hiro," like he was surprised, then opened his eyes even wider, his stark, shocked, staring eyes.

His glasses were blown away, shattered, and gone.

Blood was steadily, rhythmically pumping from a small, neat hole in his forehead, right between his eyes. Blood filled his eye sockets. He changed from Jin Rin to a monster I never knew.

I had no time to think about what had just happened, for in that instant a dark shadow filled the foxhole. I scrambled up the steep sides of the foxhole, only to fall back into the bottom, now filling with Jin

Rin's steaming red blood.

As I looked up, a man dressed in camouflage holding a rifle cautiously crept up and stood at the edge of the foxhole, looking down at me. Beside him was a large dark dog silently staring at me, his lips pulled back, showing dagger gleaming ivory teeth. He was growling, rumbling deeply. He was obviously well trained, for he didn't move a muscle, just stared at me like he would tear my face off if I tried to run.

"Kaiser, stay," the man said softly. His voice sounded kind.

It was between me and the other dog. I started to piss, even though I didn't want to. I was so frightened by what was happening.

Pissing I normally did in private, but I was completely unhinged. We dogs piss to proudly mark our territory, to let other dogs know that we owned a spot, but any dog that smelled this piss would have one thought: this dog was scared witless, and so I was. I surely didn't mark this spot because I owned it.

I growled ferociously, screaming really, baring my teeth, barking my most horrible bark. Kaiser didn't move.

"The only good Nip, so they say, is a dead one, and this is a good Nip. Got him between the eyes. I just aimed between the glasses. That's what gave him away, the moon's reflection from the glasses. Like two silver dollars gleaming bright and round, like twin flashlights. If the moon hadn't broken out at that exact moment, I might be the dead one. I sure as hell couldn't see that foxhole. Hey Mud Hole, come here, take a gander. You want his gold teeth? A rich Nip."

The man started to laugh, then stopped. He called to another man with a radio on his back,

"Hey Nez, get over here. There's a little

white dog still alive, in with the dead Japs."

"I wouldn't want to touch that little fellow," chuckled Nez. "He looks meaner than snot. What the hell? There is another dog in there as well. He looks dead, though. He is so muddy and wet I can't tell what kind of dog he is."

"Big son of a bitch, though," Chuck said. "I used to have a dog like that up in the High Sierras."

"The hell you say?" Mud Hole said.

They talked and of course I couldn't understand a word they said. I thought I had met the Hakujin, the white devils. I had met the enemy, and could now say they smelled, they stunk, they were loud, and surprisingly not threatening, though they had me scared witless, as I said. I felt exhausted and bone weary.

Just as I was thinking about how to make another leap out of that foxhole and escape, the big guy, Chuck, jumped down while throwing his coat over me. It was dry, warm, and stunk like sweat and tobacco. I never saw Jin Rin again, never heard Japanese, my home language, again. Put simply, I never saw Japan again.

We dogs in this world are doers and like to participate. We may not be able to speak the human language, but we have a vast language of our own that you humans can only guess at.

When all around us, we of the dog family can only guess at what it is that you humans are trying to say. Your human voice becomes to us dogs a bird cry, a groan, a scream at which meaning we can only guess. My problem was additionally vexed since I only knew Japanese.

We war dogs come from centuries of canine battles the world over, and we understand much, though we can't talk like you humans, we can and do understand you. War is in the marrow of our bones.

We often understand your feelings before you do. We dogs know your signs and hand commands, shouts, whistles, and clicks. We watch your eyes for meaning.

There is that oddity where you humans laugh, baring your teeth in a so-called friendly manner. I have seen good, even great dogs beaten to death, while their owners laughed, though that was rare. Laughing humans make me uneasy, especially when I didn't know the language.

We see your gums, we watch. In our language to bare one's teeth is to be angry.

Our hearing is very acute. You utter some words, and we are left to wonder what the meaning was.

We war dogs were superbly trained. We watched, listened for intruders, learned how to scent them, even to see snipers up in trees. We could swim, parachute out of planes, crawl into caves, attack, alert our squad, guard prisoners, carry messages and, of course, hunt and locate the enemy. We could do much, not to mention that the lamest dog could outrun any human, we were low and fast.

The night Jin Rin was killed I could hear and smell the enemy in the jungle way before Jin Rin did.

When I was unwrapped from the jacket and opened my eyes, we were in a plane. I had been in planes before; they were all noisy.

Mud Hole and Chuck, strapped into their seats, were talking. Nez was left behind at the air strip.

"Why do you suppose the Japs had so many dogs?"

"Why, you know the answer as well as I do, Mud Hole. So their men can sleep, same as us," and here he sat up straight. "They also can carry messages in the dark and kill Japs when possible."

The huge black dog named Kaiser slept

with his heavy head on his massive front paws, one of which rested on a large bone.

The plane droned on into the rainy, dank, murky night while Chuck and Mud Hole smoked cigars and talked. Chuck laughed, then paused and said,

"Hey Mud Hole, remember how Captain Carlson saw you drinking from that muddy stagnant ditch back there in New Guinea? So, what do they call you now?"

Mud Hole just laughed and held up a twisted cord bracelet strung with Jin Rin's gold teeth. They both roared, laughing.

I didn't hear the rest of the story. Besides, as I said, I could only understand Japanese anyway. I could only guess at what they said. As they mumbled and guffawed, I drifted off once again into a deep and scary sleep.

I probably kicked and barked, it was that kind of nightmare, with the face of Tenoshinshi, the Japanese Angel of Death, projected on hideous, smoking, shrunken grinning, fire-lit cannibal skulls.

"Someone will remember us," I said, "even in another time." -Sappho.

To author and artist Douglas Granum, creation is a way of life.

His inspiration is derived from his travels around the world and an appreciation of the unusual – trekking the jungles of New Guinea, enjoying plein aire painting in northern Urals of Russia, drifting down China's Yangtze River, looking at the stars in a Serengeti night sky, and commercial fishing in the storm-tossed Gulf of Alaska.

As an artist Douglas Granum works with and in various mediums including stone, metal, glass, wood, canvas, bronze and of course, writing. From creation in his studio in Southworth, Washington, his paintings, glass pieces, metal and stone sculptures can be found worldwide.

Find out more at DouglasGranum.com

Other stories by Douglas Granum:

JUDITH'S GAP

THE GERMAN MUSIC TEACHER'S COTTAGE

ALONE ON THE YELLOW STONE

DEATH AND AFTERLIFE ON EL PASEO

OFF A LIGHT

THE ROSE COVERED COTTAGE

Find out more at DouglasGranum.com